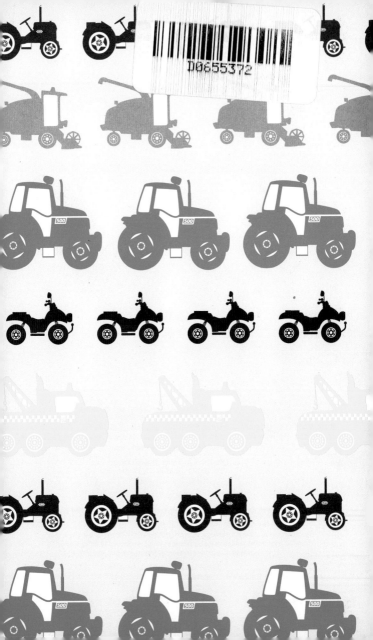

A catalogue record for this book is available from the British Library

© 2004 Little Entertainment Company Limited/Entertainment Rights PLC. All Rights Reserved.
Adapted from the television script by Keith Littler, based on the original stories by Colin Reade
Photographs by James Lampard.

Published by Ladybird Books Ltd.
80 Strand  London  WC2R 0RL
A Penguin Company

7 9 10 8 6

ISBN-13: 978-1-84422-484-5
ISBN-10: 1-8442-2484-8

Printed in China

# Gold Cup

One morning at Gosling Farm, Stan was clearing out the barn to make more room for Little Red Tractor. Hidden at the back, he found an old painting.

"That's my Granddad," said Stan to Amy and Ryan as they arrived. "He loved racing horses. He won the Babblebrook Gold Cup three times!"

"Your Granddad was a champion?" Ryan asked.

Stan laughed. "Not really, the Babblebrook Cup was a race around the farms."

"Stan, there's something stuck to the back!" said Ryan, pointing to the picture.

Stan unfolded the paper. It was a map with a big red cross on it. "That's where the old stables used to be," he said, "between Five Oaks Field and Mr Jones' land." He was puzzled. Why would his Granddad mark that on a map?

"I bet it's treasure," whispered Ryan. "Let's go and look!"

Stan shook his head. He had to deliver grain to Stumpy. "Perhaps we'll go at the weekend."

Ryan was disappointed. He and Amy waved goodbye.

On the way home, Ryan pulled the map from his pocket. Amy was shocked. The map belonged to Stan!

"I'm only borrowing it," insisted Ryan. "I just want to look at the treasure. Then I'll give the map back."

Amy thought for a moment. She imagined finding shining treasure. What an adventure! "Okay," she agreed and they both set off to Five Oaks Field.

Stan delivered the grain to Stumpy and told him about the painting.

He also asked Stumpy what had happened to the gold cup.

"I'll tell you a story about that," whispered Stumpy.

Little Red Tractor rolled his headlights with excitement.

Meanwhile, Ryan and Amy were at the edge of Five Oaks Field, next to Mr Jones' land.

"This is where the treasure's buried," said Ryan, following the map's directions.

Amy wasn't at all sure he was right, but Ryan started to dig a hole.

At the windmill, Stumpy told Stan the story of the gold cup. It had been Stan's Granddad's prized possession. He never wanted to sell it, even when times were hard.

"Your Granddad buried the cup," added Stumpy, "to save it for you."

Little Red Tractor bobbed his lights happily.
Stan was very pleased. "Come on
Little Red Tractor. It's time to go on a
treasure hunt!"

Stan jumped aboard and they set off for
Five Oaks Field.

Ryan had climbed inside the hole and tunnelled under the gate. "I've found something!" he shouted.

Amy peered into the hole. Ryan held up a mysterious bag. Just then they heard the sound of Mr Jones and Big Blue. "Honk, honk!"

Mr Jones wanted to
know what they
were doing.

"Er…digging for Stan's
treasure," squeaked Amy.

Mr Jones opened the bag.
"Well, this gold cup was
found on MY land," he
pointed out.

Big Blue honked in agreement.

Stan and Little Red Tractor arrived.

"We've found the Babblebrook gold cup!" Amy blurted out. "Mr Jones says it's his."

Stan felt really disappointed. But he saw that the cup *was* found on Mr Jones' land.

Mr Jones smiled. "You could try and win it back."

"Little Red Tractor could race Big Blue!" said Ryan.

"And the winner keeps the cup!" cheered Amy.

"Toot!" agreed Little Red Tractor.

"Honk!" agreed Big Blue.

"You're on!" Stan cried.

It was the day of the big race. Walter gave Stan his lucky hat. Stumpy held up the flag.

"Right," announced Stumpy. "Once around the field, then under the tree, through the gate and then back.

Ready ... Steady ... GO!"

Big Blue surged ahead.

"He's never going to beat us in that little tractor!" Mr Jones laughed.

Stan didn't agree. "Come on, Little Red Tractor! Let's go!" he cheered.

"Toot, toot," piped Little Red Tractor happily.

Big Blue reached the end of the field and raced up to the tree.

One of the branches was very low! Mr Jones braked and slid to a stop, just before the branch hit Big Blue.

Stan waved and Little Red Tractor tooted as they went by.

"We can still catch him, we're bigger and faster!" said Mr Jones.

Big Blue reversed and sped away from the tree. They had to beat Stan and Little Red Tractor!

Further along, Little Red Tractor hit a
bump. Stan's hat fell over his eyes.
"I can't see where I'm going!" he cried
   Little Red Tractor veered left and right.
   "Toot! Toot!" he
warned Stan.

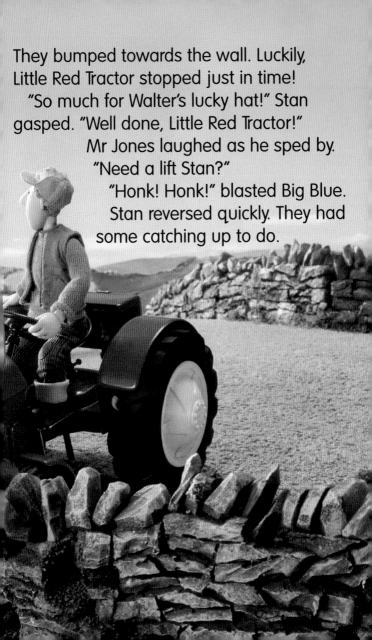

They bumped towards the wall. Luckily, Little Red Tractor stopped just in time!

"So much for Walter's lucky hat!" Stan gasped. "Well done, Little Red Tractor!"

Mr Jones laughed as he sped by.

"Need a lift Stan?"

"Honk! Honk!" blasted Big Blue.

Stan reversed quickly. They had some catching up to do.

Up ahead, Big Blue was in trouble. He couldn't fit through the single gate!

"I'll have to open the second gate too. Hang on!" cried Mr Jones.

Stan held his breath as Little Red Tractor came up to the gate. He steered around Big Blue and squeezed through!

Mr Jones watched in amazement. "We're going to be beaten by that old lump of tin!" he shouted.

"Don't forget to close the gate after you!" Stan laughed.

Stan and Little Red Tractor were winning!
Everyone cheered.

"His Granddad would be proud!"
Stumpy cried.

Little Red Tractor trundled over the finish
line, rolling his headlights.

"I knew you could do it," beamed Stan as he clutched the gold cup.

"You may not be the biggest, but you're the best!"

"Toot! Toot!" beeped a very proud Little Red Tractor.